McGrave

Lee Goldberg

A man's status in Hollywood is measured by several key indices—the sticker price of his car, the cup size of his lover's boobs, the square footage of his property, and the value of whatever he happens to collect.

By those measures, business manager Ernie Wallengren is a very important man.

He has several German luxury cars, the cheapest of which costs $120,000. His wife has enormous designer boobs and, to hedge his bets, so does his mistress. His home in the Hollywood Hills (once owned by a movie star with a raging fetish for obese women dressed in latex) is 11,500 square feet of garish excess, with more Doric columns than the Parthenon. And his collection of ceramic antiquities, much of it looted from the Middle East and bought on the black market, is world-class, if artistically unappreciated by its owner, whose personal taste runs more towards power-tool calendars. Wallengren collects the stuff just to have a valuable collection of *something*.

He protects his investment with alarms, cameras, and round-the-clock personal security, supervised by Frank Russell, a forty-four-year-old ex-LAPD detective with a waistline measurement that matches his age and a new set of teeth to replace the ones he's lost to cigarettes, Scotch, and a well-placed kick by a 210-pound tranny, a blow that had actually been aimed at his then partner, John McGrave.

It went down like this: the transsexual drug dealer took offense when McGrave happened to say, while making the arrest, that it would take more than implants, surgery, and all the estrogen on earth to make him look like a woman, much less one that anybody would want to fuck.

McGrave has a way with people.

If Russell holds a grudge against McGrave for taking that

tranny's kick, he isn't showing it tonight. He's invited McGrave over to the Wallengrens' mansion and is showing him the very old and outrageously expensive pots, plates, and cups that are on pedestals, in glass display cases, and in lighted niches all over the house.

Russell is wearing an expensive suit and shiny leather shoes. He needs to dress that way only if the Wallengrens are around, which they're not, so he's just showing off how much he makes, which would probably have been more effective if he'd left the price tags on his clothes, because McGrave doesn't know shit about fashion.

That much is obvious from what McGrave has on.

He's wearing a leather jacket that looks like it has been stained by the dribbles of a thousand greasy meals, dragged behind a car for miles, blasted with a shotgun, slashed with knives, and set on fire.

Because it has.

McGrave is wearing the story of his life over an aloha shirt and a .357 Magnum in a shoulder holster.

He's also got on the same pair of Levi's that he's been wearing all week and a dirty pair of Adidas that he's worn every day for months.

The underwear and socks are clean because McGrave never knows if he might get laid, and there's no woman, whether she's a princess or a crack whore, who isn't turned off by dirty underwear.

Russell and McGrave are standing in front of a weathered, pitted, colorless clay pot on a pedestal.

"Impressive, isn't it?" Russell says.

McGrave squints at it. "What is it?"

"The newest addition to Wallengren's collection. A three-thousand-year-old chamber pot."

"So it's a toilet," McGrave says.

"It's a rare antiquity that's worth almost half a million dollars."

McGrave shakes his head. "You gave up being a cop to guard King Tut's crapper?"

"I'm making three times as much as I did as a detective, and I'm not permanently crippled or dead, which puts me way, way ahead of all of your previous partners. And I've got a kick-ass dental plan."

Russell flashes an overly broad smile to show off his set of unnaturally straight and white teeth. They look like porcelain.

"Nice," McGrave says. "You brush those with Ty-D-Bol?"

"Very funny."

"Where is everybody?"

"The Wallengrens are in Scotland, buying a castle."

"What for?"

"I don't know, maybe so they can spend their summers taking bagpipe lessons and fishing for the Loch Ness Monster," Russell says and leads McGrave through the living room towards a set of double doors at the end of a long hallway. "The point is, half of their antiquities collection will be moved there and they're going to need someone to protect it all. You could be that man."

"No," McGrave says. "I couldn't."

Russell opens the double doors to reveal a tiny room filled with flat-screen monitors showing various angles of the interior and exterior of the house. One of the screens shows a football game on ESPN. The game is a lot more interesting to McGrave than the chamber pot.

"It's a great gig," Russell says. "Just think, you could be living in a castle on a lake with a speedboat at the dock, a sports car in the garage, a full wine cellar, and nobody around half the time. You'll live like Scottish royalty. King Sean Fucking Connery. No more days and nights on the streets, no more dealing with gangbangers, junkies, whores, pushers, and pimps."

"There goes my social life."

"I'm serious, John."

"So am I," McGrave says.

"This could be a fresh start for you. You can walk away from the job before they throw you out."

"Do you know something that I don't?"

Russell looks at him incredulously. "They call you Tidal Wave McGrave, for Christ's sake."

"Because they love me."

"Because you destroy everything and everyone in your path. It adds up. And you can bet the brass are keeping a running tab. Pretty soon they're going to decide that your clearance rate isn't worth the cost."

"So you think it would be better for me to quit now and spend my days in a closet like this."

"It's a command center," Russell says. "And you'd be in Scotland, not here. It's a great opportunity, buddy."

"What about my weekends with my daughter?"

"For one thing, she can't stand you. For another, she's going off to college in a few months. Those weekends are going to be history soon anyway."

"You've given this a lot of thought."

"We were partners. We're supposed to watch each other's backs."

McGrave nods, watching the game. "So this great opportunity to go to another continent to protect stone potties has nothing to do with you banging my ex-wife."

Russell freezes and blinks hard. He didn't see that coming. "It's not what you think."

"You aren't banging her?"

"What I mean is, it's a relationship."

"So you're banging her all the time," McGrave says, turning to Russell.

"C'mon, John, let's be reasonable about this."

"Thanks for the job offer, Frank. But I think I'll pass. I'm glad to hear about the swell dental plan, though, because I think you're gonna need it."

McGrave smiles and shoulders past Russell, who tenses up, as if expecting a blow. But McGrave keeps on walking.

Doesn't mean the blow won't come later, and Russell knows it.

Russell closes the doors, turns around, and watches the security monitors as his former partner strides out of the house, gets into his police-issue Crown Vic in the cobblestone motor court, and drives off.

Only then does Russell relax.

He sits down in a chair, takes out his cell, turns his back to the monitors, and calls McGrave's ex-wife.

"This is gonna get ugly," he says.

☙

McGrave speeds down the hill in his car, passing a Comcast cable service van parked on the street and a repair guy working at an open junction box, where he's plugged some kind of iPad-size video device into the wiring.

The repair guy is wearing an earpiece transmitter and looking intently at his iPad, where several windows are showing either an interior or exterior video feed of the Wallengren mansion.

"I'm in," the guy says in German. "Switching to recorded feed now."

☙

Russell is so involved in his phone call with McGrave's ex-wife that he doesn't notice a split-second flicker across all of the command-center screens, including the one that shows the empty entry hall, which isn't actually empty.

Two men, all muscle and sinew, and a woman with a body suitable for a successful career as an Olympic gymnast or a porn star, walk in the front door all dressed in black and wearing ski masks.

They each have earbud transmitters and are carrying matching silver cases and gym bags.

They split up, moving with silent, practiced precision into the house.

☙

Out on the street, at that open junction box, the repair guy is watching all of this go down on his iPad when someone taps him on the shoulder.

He turns and gets a fist in the face, breaking his nose like a water balloon.

It's McGrave.

If the repair guy had been more aware of his surroundings, and less focused on watching the robbery, he might have noticed that shortly after McGrave drove by, he'd made a sharp turn into a driveway just two houses down from the junction box.

McGrave punches the repair guy in the face again, mostly because it just feels so good after his conversation with Russell.

He bends down and snatches the iPad from the ground and plucks the transmitter out of the unconscious repair guy's ear and sticks it in his own.

McGrave glances at the iPad screen, toggles through the feeds, and sees the three thieves in different rooms, taking antiquities and placing them into cases lined with foam padding precut for each individual piece that they are stealing.

Pros with a shopping list.

He yanks the added wires and clips from the junction box, tosses the iPad on the ground, then opens the back of the van. The real cable guy is on the floor with a bullet in his forehead.

McGrave closes the door, takes out his cell phone, and dials Frank Russell as he hurries back down the hill to his car.

ℤ

Russell is sitting in his chair, his back to the monitors, talking to McGrave's ex, when he's interrupted by a beep.

"Hold on, baby, I'm getting another call."

He takes the phone away from his ear to look at the caller ID.

It's John McGrave.

Fuck.

He puts the phone back to his ear.

"It's him. Do you think I should take the call?"

∾

McGrave is getting into his car when one of the thieves asks him something over the transmitter in German. Not once, but twice.

So McGrave says, "*Ja wohl.*"

It's the only German he knows. It's what Sergeant Schultz said all the time to Colonel Klink on *Hogan's Heroes.*

He yanks the transmitter from his ear, takes an extra ammo clip from his glove box, and starts his car.

∾

Sebastian Richter hasn't survived and prospered as an assassin and thief simply on his intelligence, his lethal skills, and his physical prowess, though those qualities are certainly a plus on the résumé.

His edge has always been his natural predatory instincts.

And those instincts were telling him he was fucked even before McGrave said, "Yes, indeed," to him in German.

Richter drops his silver case, takes a gun out of his gym bag, and heads for the double doors of the command center.

∾

"I've got to take his call, Sharon. If I don't answer, he'll think I wet myself over his stupid threat. I got to be cool about this. Hold on," Russell says, then answers McGrave's call. "Change your mind, buddy?"

"You're being robbed," McGrave says as he's backing the car out into the street. "There are three perps in the house right now."

Russell swivels around in his chair, stands up, and looks at the monitors, where he sees rooms with empty display cases and one thin guy and one hot woman busy stealing more.

He tosses the phone on the chair and is about to slap the big red emergency button on the console when the doors behind him burst open.

Out of flawed reflex, the kind Richter has subdued in himself with years of training, Russell turns around and Richter pistol-whips him across the face, taking him down.

Richter picks up Russell's phone, looks at the caller ID, and then pockets it.

He then says this in German into his earbud: "Abort. We have a guest coming. Otto, you stop him. Serena, warm up the car."

⚭

McGrave is speeding up the street, peeling rubber on the steep grade, when the repair guy, his face splattered with blood, staggers into his path with a gun and starts shooting at him.

The windshield shatters and McGrave ducks, twisting the wheel and steering straight for the repair guy.

The car slams into the repair guy, who flies up onto the hood, through the windshield, and right into the passenger seat.

McGrave elbows the guy a few times in the face to make sure he stays down and keeps on driving, making a hard left into the Wallengrens' driveway.

⚭

Serena rushes into the Wallengrens' garage and finds two Jet Skis, a Harley-Davidson, a BMW 7 Series, and a Mercedes S-Class.

It's nice to be rich.

The keys to the vehicles are on hooks on the wall. She takes the BMW key, pops the trunk on the car, and puts her cases inside.

She pulls off her mask and throws it in, too.

Imagine the most beautiful woman you've ever seen. Now imagine one even more beautiful.

That's her.

⚭

Otto takes a defensive position at the base of the stairs in the foyer. He heard the gunshots and can now hear a car approaching fast. He removes an automatic weapon from his gym bag and aims it at the front door. He's looking forward to this. He's killed eight men and one woman in his lifetime, and those experiences are fond memories. Especially the woman.

Whoever walks in that door is a dead man.

❧

But McGrave doesn't walk in.

He drives in.

❧

The Crown Vic blasts through the front door and takes most of the wall with it, plowing over Otto before he can even squeeze the trigger.

McGrave gets out of the car in a rain of dust and debris and squints down at Otto's arm sticking out from underneath the front driver's-side wheel.

There's a colorful tattoo of a woman embracing a bear on the dead man's twitching arm. The twitching makes the tattoo look like a crudely animated cartoon.

McGrave takes out his .357 and strides casually into the living room.

He couldn't possibly be happier than he is right now.

And the feeling isn't diminished one bit when he sees Richter, his face hidden by the ski mask, standing behind Frank Russell and holding an automatic weapon to the dizzy ex-cop's head.

McGrave raises his gun and aims it at Richter, who stands across the room full of ceramic antiquities. "LAPD. Game over."

Richter cocks his head. "You're really a cop?"

"I am," McGrave says.

"Where did we go wrong?"

"You made two mistakes. Your first was using a Comcast cable truck in a Time Warner Cable neighborhood."

"I'll have to remember that next time. What was the second?"

"Picking a hostage who is screwing my wife."

McGrave fires.

The bullet smashes through the three-thousand-year-old stone toilet, obliterating it, and hits Russell in the upper chest, passing through him into Richter's shoulder.

The German tumbles backwards and fires, spraying the room with bullets.

McGrave dives to the floor as glass and ceramics explode all around him.

Richter scrambles out of the room and down a hallway. McGrave runs up and checks on Russell, who is wide awake and wishes he wasn't. His new suit is soaked with blood. At least his teeth are fine.

"Are you going to live?" McGrave asks.

"Yeah," Russell says.

"My aim must be off," McGrave says, then hurries after Richter.

⌘

The BMW is running, Serena is at the wheel, and the garage door is open as Richter staggers in, clutching his bleeding shoulder. He gets into the car. She peels out, filling the garage with smoke.

A moment later McGrave rushes in, spots the Mercedes, and grabs the key. He gets in the car and backs out fast, scraping the passenger side of the Mercedes against a pillar and shearing off the mirror.

The chase is on.

⌘

Los Angeles is the only big city that's got a small mountain range in the middle of it.

But that's part of the whole status thing. The mountains are a natural dividing line between the haves in Beverly Hills, Bel-Air, and Hancock Park on one side and the have-nots in the tract home and shopping mall wastelands of the San Fernando Valley on the other.

Mulholland Drive is a two-lane, serpentine road that runs along the crest of the mountains and is named after the guy who built a two-hundred-mile aqueduct to drain water from the Northern California delta down to Los Angeles just so developers could get rich building homes in a place that otherwise is inhospitable to human life.

The whole city is a carefully constructed lie built on greed.

So now you know why they make so many movies, television shows, and fighter jets here.

And why Los Angeles has more plastic surgeons per capita than anywhere else on earth.

§

Serena is not only beautiful, but she can drive.

She heads up the hill to Mulholland, then weaves through the traffic at an insane speed, deftly avoiding cars going in both directions without hitting the hillside on her left or going off the cliff on her right.

She makes it look easy.

McGrave is coming up fast behind them, weaving wildly around cars, going in and out of oncoming traffic, scraping the hillside and the guardrail.

He makes it look scary.

"Who is that guy?" Serena asks in German.

Richter takes off his mask and looks over his shoulder as McGrave sideswipes the car Serena just avoided in his zeal to catch up to them.

"A dead man," Richter says.

Serena passes an SUV that's in front of them and, as she does,

11

Richter leans out the window and shoots out the SUV's tires.

The SUV spins out of control, right across McGrave's path.

He swerves into the other lane, clipping the spinning SUV with his front passenger-side bumper.

The impact triggers his air bags.

He keeps on going, pedal to the floor, even though he can't see a thing with the bag in his face.

The car scrapes the guardrail, shooting off sparks, as he heads towards a hairpin turn.

⌘

Serena is already in the turn, swerving into the opposite lane to pass a slow car in front of her.

She doesn't see the Hollywood Celebrity Homes Tour bus coming around the bend until it's too late.

Serena jerks the wheel hard to the right to avoid a head-on collision and tries to squeeze between the bus and the guardrail.

And gets rear-ended by the car she just passed.

She loses control, smashes through the guardrail, and goes off the cliff.

The BMW flies into the night sky and then drops into the deep canyon below.

⌘

McGrave pushes the air bag out of his way, sees the curve and the bus coming at him, and wrenches the steering wheel hard to the left at the last possible second.

The bus grinds to a stop, brakes squealing like pigs.

McGrave spins and ends across the lanes. The bus hits the passenger side of his car, shattering his windows, buckling his dashboard, and snapping the burled walnut trim. The side air bags all go off.

He scrambles out of the crumpled Mercedes and staggers to

the broken guardrail just in time to see the BMW swallowed by the dark depths of the canyon below.

⋐⋑

Captain Roy Thackery has been a cop for twenty-five years and has a nice side gig working as a technical consultant on one of those TV series where the cops do autopsies themselves, wear Armani suits, drive vintage muscle cars, live on the beach, and can access the cameras on spy satellites with their cell phones.

He answers incredibly stupid questions from the writers, offers them "authentic cop talk" that he totally makes up, and shares outrageously embellished anecdotes from the cases he's worked.

The producers think that his input gives their show its "gritty verisimilitude," as if having their ex-stripper turned Navy SEAL turned homicide detective character say a few words from an actual cop makes her any more believable than, say, a talking goldfish who solves crimes.

But for his $500 an episode, he's glad to tell them that it does.

What he really wants is to write an episode himself. That's a $30,000 payday, not including residuals, and he figures if his script is any good, it could lead to something more, like maybe a producing gig, maybe a series of his own someday.

So what he needs is quiet time to write. No distractions. No controversies. A clear head so he can create.

What he gets is John McGrave engaging in a shoot-out and a pursuit that shuts down Mulholland Drive in both directions at nine p.m. on a Saturday night.

⋐⋑

The scene of the crash is illuminated by portable lights. News choppers swarm overhead, kicking up the air and blowing dust around. Police officers and crime scene investigators scurry around measuring things, bagging stuff, writing notes, and taking pictures.

Paramedics treat the drivers of the crashed cars and the tourists in the bus for their mild injuries and what will later be characterized by their attorneys as "severe infliction of emotional distress."

McGrave stands at the cliff's edge, drinking a Hawaiian Punch and eating Oreos that he mooched from a paramedic who keeps the stuff around to treat people for shock. He's watching a crane drag the wrecked BMW up from the canyon below. Firemen move through the brush, looking for anything that might spark a blaze.

Captain Thackery joins him and reeks of spearmint. Ever since he quit smoking, he's always got a mint in his mouth. He's like a highly evolved Altoid.

"What brings you out here, Roy?" McGrave says.

"Jesus Christ, McGrave," Thackery says. "You drove a car through a house, shot up a collection of rare artifacts, stole a Mercedes, ran it into two cars, chased another one off a cliff, and then crashed into a bus full of tourists."

"Yeah. So?"

"What were you thinking?"

"That I wanted to catch the bad guys," McGrave says.

"And as a result, you made things far worse than they would have been if you'd just let the thieves get away with the crime."

"Do nothing. Now that's an innovative approach to law enforcement that I've never considered before. Is that how you got ahead, Roy? Because I've always wondered what your secret was."

"Do you see the news choppers up there? You shut down Mulholland Drive. It's all over the news. And since the crash, those tourists in the bus have already sent out a thousand e-mails, tweets, photos, and videos of this fiasco to the entire planet. There's going to be lots of heat on this, so you'd better hope that all of your extreme actions tonight were justified."

McGrave nods. "Is the phony cable guy talking?"

"Only to St. Peter."

The instant Thackery says it, he knows it's a good line, one they'd love on the show. But he doesn't want to reach for his notebook, because that would be so fucking obvious.

"Go ahead, write it down," McGrave says.

"Fuck you," Thackery says, but he takes out his pad and makes the note anyway, deciding as he does that he ought to start carrying a little digital recorder around to capture his gems of authentic cop talk.

The BMW is brought to the street.

The car is pancaked.

McGrave goes over and peers inside. Serena is still buckled into her seat, her head twisted at an angle not compatible with living. Her eyes are wide open and look like fogged glass.

The passenger seat is empty.

There could be a corpse in the brush at the bottom of the canyon, but McGrave knows in his gut that there isn't.

He goes back to the cliff's edge and looks out at the glittering lights of the San Fernando Valley.

The bastard is out there somewhere. And McGrave is going to find him.

∾

It's a warm, sunny Sunday morning, which is another way of saying there's a stage-two smog alert and Los Angeles residents are strongly advised to stay indoors and not breathe more than is absolutely necessary.

McGrave is at his cluttered cubicle, studying a coroner's photo of Otto's tattoo and talking on the phone.

He asks the watch commander in the North Hollywood station to:

1. Send some patrol cars around to the local Laundromats and see if anybody has complained that some of their laundry is missing or if they've seen a guy who looks like he was shot and thrown off a cliff.

2. Get him a list of any cars reported stolen in the area since nine p.m. The same goes for any reports of break-ins at homes, drugstores, or doctors' offices.

McGrave figures that when the German staggers out of the hills, he's going to want clothes that aren't soaked with blood, a car to get as far from the area as possible, and drugs to kill the pain and prevent infection.

The watch commander agrees to help.

McGrave hangs up and catches a whiff of spearmint in the air, so he starts delivering his update on the case even before Captain Thackery shows up at his cubicle.

"I ran the faces and prints of the three dead thieves past U.S. Customs. Turns out they arrived from Berlin on three separate flights over the last two days. Customs has double-checked the passports. They're fakes."

The captain leans on the wobbly, chest-high wall of McGrave's cubicle and swallows his mint.

"I just got off the phone with the chief, who has already heard from Wallengren's attorney," Thackery says. "Tomorrow they're going to file a lawsuit against the city for twenty million dollars in damages."

"That much? I've got to hold on to my toilet," McGrave says. "In three thousand years, it could be worth a fortune."

"There's more. Frank Russell wants you arrested for attempted murder. He says you shot him because he's sleeping with your ex."

"I shot Frank to nail the guy who was holding a gun to his head."

"The security camera footage and audio strongly back Frank's side of the story. The DA is taking this very seriously and is contemplating charges. But the chief isn't waiting for the DA's decision. He wants you off the street now."

"You're suspending me?"

"I'm firing you. You have twenty minutes to clean out your desk and get the hell out of here."

"You can't just fire me, Roy. There's a whole bunch of tedious, bureaucratic crap you have to go through first, hearings and review boards and that kind of thing. It'll be weeks, maybe months, before you can actually fire me. So in the meantime, I'll catch the bastard responsible for all of this and everything will be fine."

"You don't get it, McGrave. It's a done deal. The city is tired of getting sued every time you step out of the building. I'm tired of the aggravation. And you won't find any support with your union rep. They're standing behind Frank on this one."

"Looks like your 'do nothing' approach to policing is catching on," McGrave says. "I guess this means I can't count on you as a reference."

"I'd look into a new profession, because you're finished as a cop in this city or anywhere else. No police force is going to hire you with lawsuits and criminal charges hanging over your head. Leave your gun and your badge on my desk before you go."

The captain walks away.

McGrave is just beginning to absorb the magnitude of what has happened to him when his cell phone rings. He grabs it and answers out of reflex.

"McGrave," he says.

"She was the only woman who was ever more to me than a warm body in my bed."

McGrave sits up straight in his chair, his professional problems forgotten.

It's the German.

જ

It's a cramped little bathroom with bloody towels on the linoleum floor, a bloody pair of needle-nose pliers in the blood-splashed sink, and a bloody bullet in the bloody soap dish.

Perhaps you're sensing a theme here.

Richter stands in front of the mirror in a clean but oversize white shirt, his left arm in a crude sling fashioned from a towel. He's studying his reflection and holding a portable home phone in his good hand. He's clean-shaven and his hair is washed, but his skin is a sickly pale and his brow is already dappled with perspiration.

But considering that he just dug a bullet out of his shoulder with pliers, doused the wound with rubbing alcohol, and stitched it shut with dental floss, he looks fucking great.

"She died with her eyes open," he says. "Did you look into them, McGrave?"

⌯

McGrave looks at the caller ID on his phone.

It reads "John McGrave." The son of a bitch is in his house.

"Yeah, I did," McGrave says.

"Then you know what I am going to see when I look into your eyes at the end of our next encounter."

⌯

Richter opens the medicine cabinet behind the mirror, sorts through the prescription medication until he finds what he wants. Vicodin. He pockets it.

"It's a date," McGrave says. "Make yourself comfy. I'll be home in ten minutes."

Richter steps into the bedroom. The bed is unmade. The furniture looks like it was bought used from a Motel 6. He glances at a framed photo on the dresser of McGrave, his ex-wife, and his teenage daughter, all of them soaking wet and laughing as they try to wash an uncooperative bulldog in a plastic kiddie pool.

"You have a nice family. I'll be back for them, too."

He tosses the phone on the bed and steps over the carcass of the bulldog, a kitchen knife buried to the hilt in its throat, as he walks out.

⌯

Whoever designed Berlin-Tegel Airport had a fetish for hexagons. The terminal is shaped like a hexagon. The pillars are hexagons. The floor tiles are hexagons. The ceiling lights are part of a gridwork of interlocking hexagons. Outside, there are hexagonal concrete benches on a hexagonal-patterned sidewalk bordering a hexagonal parking lot.

The architect probably slept in a hexagonal bed in a hexagonal apartment and made his girlfriend wear hexagonal underwear.

But the hexagons go unnoticed by John McGrave as he emerges from the terminal into the chilly Berlin night carrying only an overstuffed gym bag.

He's a man on a mission.

McGrave stands out in the crowd of stylishly dressed and stylishly disinterested Europeans. He is wearing a beat-up leather jacket, a loud Hawaiian shirt, faded jeans, and dirty tennis shoes. And yes, they're the same clothes he was wearing on Saturday. Be glad you weren't the passenger sitting next to him in coach on the fourteen-hour flight, because he hasn't shaved, or bathed, in almost two days.

He approaches a line of tan E-Class Mercedes sedans idling at the curb. The driver of the first car, a short Turkish man with a thin mustache, steps forward and reaches for McGrave's bag. But McGrave holds it out of reach.

"No, thanks," McGrave says. "I want a taxi."

The driver gestures to his car. "This is a taxi."

"That's a limo. I want a taxi."

The driver points to the other Mercedes behind his. "All taxis."

"Do I look like I can afford a ride like that? Forget the *der* limo. I want the *der* taxi. Where are the *der* taxis?"

Again, the driver points to the other Mercedes. "Here. There. All taxis."

"Okay, I see them," McGrave says. "Now show me where I can find the cheap ones."

Ladies and gentlemen, Tidal Wave is in Berlin.

⁂

During the Cold War, the shopping district of Kurfürstendamm, known by locals as the Ku'damm, was a garish, glittering, glaring beacon of conspicuous consumption, shining bright from the walled island of Capitalism that was surrounded by the red sea of Communist East Germany.

But since the wall fell, all the action has moved to Mitte, the reinvigorated heart of old Berlin, and the Ku'damm has had to change. Its vibrancy today comes less from the big stores, fancy restaurants, historic relics, and tourist traps on the main thoroughfare than from the eclectic mix of cafés, galleries, "sex kinos," boutiques, and bars to be found on the side streets.

One such place is Der Reizvolle Bar. The exterior embodies the contrasts of the Ku'damm. It has a tasteful, marble-tiled exterior and a garish, well-lit sign depicting a buxom woman hugging a grinning bear.

Der Reizvolle, by the way, is German for "Sexy Bear." And yeah, that sign looks just like the tattoo on Otto's arm.

Across the street from Der Reizvolle is a panel van, a vehicle favored as much by thieves robbing homes in the Hollywood Hills as by police officers involved in surveillance operations.

Two such police officers happen to be sitting in the back of this van, facing a monitor mounted on the wall that shows a wide-angle view of the exterior of the club.

The thin young cop with the prematurely receding hairline and the big goatee that he hopes will distract you from it, and who is presently second-guessing the wisdom of piercing his nipple two weeks ago to impress his girlfriend, is Kriminalkommissar Stefan Krementz.

The fat older one, with the rosy cheeks and an undiagnosed thyroid condition that makes his eyes bulge from his chubby face, and who is happily slurping up the Dreistern Hausmacher Gulasch, halb und halb, aus Schweine und Rindfleisch that he is digging out of a can with a spoon, is Kriminalkommissar Heinrich Bader.

Stefan looks at the slop his partner is eating. "What is that? Dog food?"

"It's a delicacy from the old GDR. I buy it over the Internet."

"The wall fell so you'd have the freedom not to eat that crap anymore," Stefan says.

"The wall fell so the West could sell us more expensive crap to eat."

Stefan spots something on the monitor. "Hello."

An old rusted Volkswagen taxi-van chugs up outside of Der Reizvolle. The taxi is rattling and spewing smoke. John McGrave emerges with his suitcase, looks around, and goes inside the club.

Stefan looks at Heinrich. "Who is that?"

"You're familiar with the phrase 'Ugly Americans'?"

"Yeah."

Heinrich tosses his empty can on the floor. "Now you know where it comes from."

&

The Sexy Bear Club is all chrome, neon, and skin. The music is loud, throbbing, and percussive. The clientele is upscale, fashionable, and almost exclusively male. The four dancing girls on the stage are topless, black haired, self-possessed, and arrogant, wearing G-strings and high heels, moving in unison to a well-choreographed routine. The only thing missing is Robert Palmer's reanimated corpse and it would be the 1980s all over again.

McGrave approaches the crowded bar and its neon-trimmed shelves of fine spirits. He takes a stool at the corner, sets down his suitcase, and waves over the bartender. She's a short-haired blonde wearing a low-cut red bandage dress that hugs her curves so tightly that she makes that blue babe Mystique in the *X-Men* look like she's got on a parka.

Maria is wearing a necklace with a pointed silver pendant that's like an arrow pointing at her deep cleavage, and McGrave follows the directions.

"Nice rack," McGrave says.

"*Danke*," she says.

"I meant the neon." He smiles and gestures to the lighted

shelves behind her.

"Now I'm hurt." Her English is perfect and only slightly accented.

"What's your name?"

"Maria. What can I get you, big guy?"

"Diet Coke. In the bottle."

She gets him a bottle, sets it in front of him, and pops the top. She starts to go.

"One more thing. You see that big ugly bruiser over there?"

He tips his bottle towards the muscled guy in the tight black T-shirt at the other end of the bar, who is watching the customers near the stage instead of the dancers. Obviously, he's a bouncer.

"That is Dieter," she says. "What about him?"

"Give him this." McGrave hands her a photo of Otto's corpse on a morgue slab.

Maria looks at it, then back at him, shocked. "Are you sure?"

"Yeah," he says and takes a sip of Diet Coke.

"That's Otto Stoffmacher, one of the owners of this club," she says. "Dieter and Otto are friends."

"Show him," McGrave says.

She hesitates but delivers the photo to the bouncer. McGrave takes out a roll of Mentos from his pocket as he watches her go.

Dieter looks at the photo, blinks hard, and then glowers at McGrave, who smiles and waves.

The bouncer steps away from the bar and disappears into a back room.

Maria returns to McGrave, who unwraps the Mentos. "You should leave while you still have a pulse."

He spills a couple of Mentos on the counter and eats one. "Don't worry, Maria. I know what I'm doing. You can relax, and so can your friends outside."

She looks at him quizzically, but before she can say anything, Dieter returns with a burly guy in a suit that can barely hold all his muscles. Dieter steps up close to McGrave. Burly sends Maria away with a sharp glance, then slaps the photo down hard on the counter in front of McGrave.

"What happened to him?" Burly asks.

"He met me," McGrave says. "Would you like to meet me?"

"*Ja*. Very much."

Burly opens his jacket so McGrave can see the gun shoved under his waistband.

"That's real terrifying and all," McGrave says, "but what happens if you have to bend over and tie your shoe?"

"Come with us," Burly says. It's an order, not an invitation.

Dieter cracks his knuckles for emphasis.

"Sure," McGrave says.

He drops his Mentos into his bottle of Diet Coke and walks away from the bar. An instant later, the bottle explodes, spewing an enormous geyser of foam, startling everyone in the place but McGrave, who uses the distraction to take Burly's gun, elbow Dieter hard in the throat, and knock Burly to the floor.

The dancers stop dancing. Everyone turns and stares. But the music is still playing and it actually isn't a bad soundtrack for what is going down.

McGrave puts the gun in Burly's face with one hand and holds up his badge with the other for everyone in the place to see, especially Maria.

"LAPD. Everybody take it easy."

McGrave glances at Dieter, who is wide-eyed, gurgling, and desperately clutching his throat, and decides the bouncer presents no threat. He looks down at Burly.

"Who was the dead guy to you?"

"My partner in this club," Burly says.

"What was he doing in Los Angeles?"

"Vacation."

McGrave shoots the floor next to Burly's head. People drop down and take cover. Others scramble for the door.

Maria tenses up, but her gaze drifts to a well-dressed man in a perfectly tailored Brioni suit sitting alone and stock-still at a table, holding his glass. He looks like a male model advertising whiskey.

"Try again," McGrave says to Burly.

"On a job. With the man."

"What man?"

Maria is paying no attention to McGrave. She's watching the well-dressed customer, who is glancing furtively at the back door.

"I don't know his name," Burly says.

McGrave presses the gun to Burly's forehead and cocks the trigger. "How do I find him?"

Burly spits it out in a panic. "You don't. He finds you. He has an agent, Hans Beimler. You meet Beimler. If he likes the job, he sets up a meet with the man."

"Where's Beimler?"

"Tequila's. On the beach at Mühlenstrasse."

The well-dressed man bolts for the back door. Maria leaps over the bar, no mean feat in her dress, and runs across the club after him, holding her pendant to her mouth and talking into it.

"*Verdammt! Schmidt rennt. Alle Einheiten rein! Los!*"

McGrave runs after her, going out the back door just as Stefan, Heinrich, and dozens of uniformed *Polizei* in their green uniforms swarm in.

&

The well-dressed man gets into a four-door Porsche Panamera parked in the back alley and drives off.

Marie curses and dashes to a tiny dented Opel Astra that's not half as nice, or as aerodynamic, as the trash Dumpster that it's parked beside. She starts the car and is about to go when McGrave hops into the passenger seat.

"Detective John McGrave, LAPD." He clips his badge to a chain around his neck and smiles at her.

She glares at him. "Kriminalkommissar Maria Vogt, Berlin Polizei."

She floors it.

❀

The Porsche speeds out onto the grand tree-lined boulevard, the Opel right behind it. The two cars weave through the traffic on the Ku'damm, past the posh shops, the gourmet restaurants, and the wooden kiosks that sell tourist trinkets.

Maria drives with concentration and skill, using the manual transmission like a pro. The Opel has more guts under the hood than McGrave would ever have guessed.

"What are you doing in Berlin?" she asks.

"A takedown crew from here blew a heist in LA. The crew got killed, the leader got away. I think he's back here now," McGrave says, keeping his eye on the Porsche. "So who are we chasing?"

"Arno Schmidt, an international drug trafficker."

McGrave nods. "Cool."

God, she hates this guy. "How did you know I was a police officer?"

"That's like asking how I know you're a woman."

"It's that obvious?"

He glances at her and lets his gaze drift up and down her body. "Abundantly."

"*Arschloch*," she says.

"What does that mean?"

"It's German for 'thank you.'"

The Porsche is ahead of them but getting bogged down in the traffic. Maria steers the Opel up onto the sidewalk, leaning on her horn to warn people, who scatter out of her path.

She gains on the Porsche. "You knew you'd find a cop inside."

"I spotted the surveillance outside the strip club, so I knew the cop inside would be the woman wearing the most clothes."

That doesn't make her feel any better. "This undercover operation took six months to set up and you ruined it in sixty seconds. What brought you to the club?"

"Otto's tattoo. He was one of the thieves in the crew."

"So that's why he invested in the club. He was using it to

launder the money he got from his share of the stolen goods."

"I showed a picture of the tattoo to my taxi driver and he recognized it as the sign for the club."

Maria closes in on the driver's side of Schmidt's Porsche. She reaches behind her seat and hands McGrave a white paddle with a red reflector in the middle. There are two words on the paddle: "HALT POLIZEI."

McGrave gives it a look. "Are you inviting me to play Ping-Pong?"

"It's an *Anhaltekelle*."

"Okay," he says. "What am I supposed to do with it?"

"When I get alongside Schmidt's car, hold it out your window."

"Why?"

She looks at him as if he's just asked her why people breathe. "So he'll stop."

"Why the hell would he do that?"

"Just do it," she snaps.

McGrave shrugs and rolls down his window.

Maria pulls up alongside the Porsche's open driver's-side window. McGrave holds the paddle out the window and throws it at Schmidt's head.

⁊

The paddle hits Schmidt on the temple and instantly knocks him out cold.

At the wheel of a speeding car.

Warning: Driving while unconscious is extremely hazardous. Do not try this at home.

⁊

Schmidt's car veers off the road, hits the median, and flips over, spiraling through the air and landing upside down on the street again . . .

. . . and sliding into an unoccupied kiosk of souvenirs, demolishing it in an explosion of wood, glass, concrete, key chains, snow globes, beer mugs, T-shirts, banners, postcards, plates, teddy bears, keepsake chips of the Berlin Wall, and a fine dust of cocaine.

☙

Maria skids to a stop. The trunk of Schmidt's car has popped open, spilling bags of cocaine onto the sidewalk, where several of them have burst apart.

McGrave looks at Maria and nods. "What do you know? The paddle works."

☙

The *Polizei Hauptsitz* is in an old stone building with turrets that once housed soldiers. The gravel-covered, sparsely landscaped grounds are encircled by tall brick walls topped with razor wire.

The exterior is colorful, welcoming, and chock-full of curb appeal compared to the soul-crushing interior of the place. The walls are a faded green, the ceiling covered with water-stained acoustic tiles, and the dangling panels of fluorescent lights cast everything in a piss-yellow hue.

The little natural light that comes through is filtered through windows that are permanently fogged by decades of snow, rain, and heat that have scratched the surface and baked layers of dirt and bird crap into the glass.

The metal desks that are crammed into the narrow squad room date back decades and could qualify as genuine historical artifacts from the GDR.

Kriminalhauptkommissar Torsten Schneider could, too.

He's in his late fifties, old enough to remember what it was like to live in the East and to dream about the West, but young enough that when the wall fell he was able to deftly adapt to the cataclysmic cultural and political changes that unification wrought.

Torsten was a very different cop in the GDR then than he is now, but he has no regrets, no hidden shame.

Although East Germany is gone, he hasn't lost his yearning for the idealized West of his youth, which he imagines still exists across the Atlantic, mostly because he's never left Europe.

Torsten is a short, stocky man who tries to hide his baldness with a comb-over that fools no one, not even himself. He sits at his desk, reading Maria Vogt's report of what happened at Der Reizvolle Bar.

Maria stands dutifully and self-consciously in front of him, dressed now in a V-neck sweater over a T-shirt, a leather jacket, and jeans.

Rather than stare at Torsten while he reads, Maria's gaze shifts from the cowboy hat on his coatrack, to the faded *Cahill: U.S. Marshal* movie poster thumbtacked on the wall, to his stack of American country-western CDs on top of his file cabinet.

Torsten turns a page on the report. "He blew up his cola with a mint?"

She nods and clears her throat. "It's a chemical process known as nucleation, sir. The glazed surface of the mint causes the carbon dioxide in the liquid to—"

Torsten interrupts her, turning another page. "He threw the *Anhaltekelle* at Schmidt and caused a major car crash on Kurfürstendamm?"

"I'm afraid so, sir," she says. "Schmidt has a serious concussion, but it could have been much worse, which is why I think—"

Torsten interrupts her again, closing the file. "Astonishing!"

"Indeed it is, sir." She takes his reaction as a very good sign. It means McGrave is taking the heat for the debacle and not her. "I suggest we put McGrave on the first plane back to Los Angeles."

But Torsten is not listening to her. "I wish I had ten more like him."

Marie blinks hard. "Sir?"

He gets up from his desk and marches out into the squad room. "I have to meet this man."

Maria follows him, bewildered.

☙

McGrave is leaning back in a chair, his feet up on Maria's desk, sound asleep and lightly snoring. He's still wearing his badge, and there are the remains of a McDonald's meal on the blotter by his feet: the to-go bags, three Big Mac cartons, a few scattered French fries, some pieces of lettuce, a crushed ketchup packet.

Stefan and Heinrich are studying McGrave from the vantage point of their side-by-side desks, a few feet away.

"Why do the American police wear their badges around their necks like jewelry?" Stefan asks in German, just in case McGrave can hear him.

"Because they are all homosexuals," Heinrich says.

Torsten and Maria walk up and stand in front of McGrave. Torsten shakes McGrave's foot. McGrave opens one eye.

"Detective McGrave, I'm Kriminalhauptkommissar Torsten Schneider, but my friends call me Duke." He offers McGrave his hand.

McGrave sits up with a yawn, swings his feet off the desk, and shakes Torsten's hand. "Why? Are you some kind of German royalty?"

"I remind people of John Wayne."

McGrave gives him a once-over, glances at Maria, then says, "I definitely see the resemblance. Not so much in physical stature, but in the confident way you carry yourself."

Maria groans, but Torsten grins with pleasure. "I run the *Schwerstkriminalitat*, our Major Crimes Unit. You only arrived hours ago and I'm already stunned by how much you've accomplished."

"I think you mean *demolished*, sir," Maria says.

Torsten gives her a sharp look. "I know what I mean, Frau Kommissar. You didn't have a court order to search Schmidt's car. However, thanks to Detective McGrave's decisive action, we have Schmidt and the cocaine, which we can use as leverage to get him to testify against the rest of the cartel." He turns now to McGrave. "How can we assist you in return, Detective?"

"You could find my suitcase, for starters."

Torsten glances at Stefan and Heinrich. "Do you have it?"

"It's gone, Herr Hauptkommissar," Stefan says. "Stolen in the chaos at the club."

"Then we must recover it," Torsten says.

Heinrich takes out a notepad and looks at McGrave. "Were there any identifiable belongings of value in your suitcase?"

"Just my lucky jockstrap," McGrave says. They stare at him. They have no clue what he is talking about. "Never mind. What can you tell me about Hans Beimler?"

Maria extracts a file from underneath the McDonald's wrappers on her desk, shakes some ketchup off of it, and opens it.

"When obscenely wealthy collectors find something they want that can't be bought, they go to Herr Beimler. He finds the right thief for the heist and takes a commission."

"You got a mug shot on this guy?" he asks.

She opens the file and hands him a photo, which he glances at, then puts in his pocket. "What do you intend to do with that?"

"I'm going to the beach to see Beimler and convince him to lead me to the mastermind behind the LA job," McGrave says, then turns to Torsten. "I could use your best man, someone who really knows the streets, to act as my driver, translator, and guide to the Berlin underworld."

Torsten claps Maria on the back. "Done!"

☙

Maria is in hell. She'd rather be assigned as bait for the pickpockets and perverts at the train station than spend another hour with John McGrave.

She's known him only a few hours and already hates him.

☙

Maria and McGrave emerge from the back of the building into the parking lot, where there is a fleet of green-and-white patrol cars, all of them BMW 5 Series sedans.

"Damn." McGrave stops and admires one of the patrol cars. "Now, this is a country that truly appreciates their police force."

"You haven't seen my paycheck," she says.

"You don't know how lucky you are." McGrave peers in the driver's-side window of the BMW. "Where I come from, a cop can only dream of owning a car like this, and you get to drive one every day."

"I don't. Only the uniformed patrol officers do."

"So what's a detective drive?" McGrave asks. "A Maserati? A Ferrari? A Bentley?"

"I'll show you." She leads him to the other side of the building to a lot containing compact Opel Astras and Volkswagen Passats. "Take your pick."

"You're kidding me," McGrave says, clearly disappointed. "These aren't much more than golf carts."

She goes to a Passat and opens the trunk. "Before we go to the beach, there's something you need to understand."

"Yeah, why taxi drivers have Mercedes, patrolmen have BMWs, and detectives drive soup cans."

She has no patience for his shit.

"It has been a long, difficult, and painful struggle to get where I am. Now I have a good chance at being promoted to *Oberkommissar* and I will not let you or your case ruin that for me. Do we understand each other?"

She gives him a hard look. He holds up his hands in surrender.

"I'll be on my very best behavior," he says.

"Great," she says. "You can begin by giving me your gun."

"It's in my sock drawer in LA," McGrave says.

"I'm referring to the one that you took at the club," she says, "and that is now hidden under your jacket."

"Oh. That gun." He reaches under his jacket, and behind his back, and hands the gun to her. "I thought of it more as a souvenir."

"You can have this instead." She puts the gun in a locker in the trunk and hands him a teddy bear dressed in a green *Polizei* uniform and cap.

"What's this?" he asks.

"Bulli the Bear. We keep them in our vehicles to give to children involved in car accidents. You definitely qualify."

Maria slams the trunk closed and gets in the car. McGrave tosses the bear and gets in the passenger side.

☙

Mühlenstrasse is a wide street that runs along the industrial, east side of the Spree River, a waterway that neatly divided Berlin seven hundred years ago and then again when the wall went up along the shore.

Although the wall fell nearly thirty years ago, the two sides of the rivers are still worlds apart.

On the western side, there are gleaming new office towers and, just as tall and rising out of the water, there are three enormous statues of male silhouettes riddled with holes.

By comparison, the eastern shore is lined with empty warehouses, empty lots, and bleak, boxy, Communist-era apartment houses.

The only cultural contribution the east bank has to offer is a half-mile, mural-covered remnant of the Berlin Wall that separates Mühlenstrasse from the river. The murals are faded, peeling, and covered with graffiti.

Maria parks a few yards away from the most famous mural, depicting Brezhnev and Honecker in a lip-mashing kiss. McGrave has no idea who the old men in suits are or why they are kissing, which tells you all you need to know about the state of the education system in California in the 1980s.

She and McGrave get out of the car. She's thankful for the fresh air. He smells like a homeless person and looks like one, too.

McGrave surveys the dismal boulevard and the wall that blocks his view of the river.

"This doesn't look like much of a resort."

"It's not," she says. "This is the former East Germany. You're looking at the longest surviving section of the Berlin Wall. Now it's an outdoor art gallery."

"So where's the beach?"

She gestures to a doorway cut into the wall and leads him through it.

They emerge onto a narrow strip of sand on the riverbank that's littered with cigarette butts and bottle caps and cluttered with folding picnic tables under yellow Corona beer umbrellas. Several ratty canvas-and-wood lawn chairs are scattered about, occupied by a dozen pale people sunning themselves.

Tequila's is a snack shack made of weathered timber and corrugated metal and festooned with banners, a poor but enthusiastic attempt to evoke a Mexican cantina.

A short jetty leads to a rusted barge carpeted with Astroturf and covered with plastic chaise lounges, picnic tables, and beach umbrellas, where a handful of people are drinking beers and eating bowls of tortilla chips.

McGrave grimaces as if the sight is causing him physical pain. "You call this a beach?"

"It is more than that," she says.

"It looks like a lot less to me."

"Before the wall fell, this was a no-man's-land between repression and freedom, watched over by guards in gun towers and patrol boats," she says. "Now it is a place where people can play and relax. Surely you can appreciate the symbolic value."

"Sure. Its mud with some sand spread on top. Very moving."

McGrave scans the pale bodies and spots Beimler on the barge.

Beimler is shirtless, wearing a pair of loud, floral board shorts and sitting alone at a table, sipping a beer and talking on his cell phone. He looks like Jabba the Hutt after gastric bypass surgery.

McGrave marches down the gangplank to the barge, Maria right behind him.

He strides up to Beimler's table. "Hey, Hans, how's it hanging?"

Beimler ends his call and says, "*Ich spreche nicht Englisch.*"

McGrave has no idea what that means and doesn't care. "There's a Rembrandt I saw over in the Louvre that I think would look just fabulous hanging in my apartment. You know anybody who can steal it for me?"

Beimler looks at him blankly with his shar-pei face.

Maria turns to McGrave. "He doesn't speak English."

"My ass," McGrave says.

"In case you haven't noticed, McGrave, you're in a foreign country. People aren't required to be fluent in English. How many languages do you know?"

"The only one that counts."

Maria sighs. This is going to be a long fucking day.

She flashes her ID at Beimler, introduces herself, and proceeds to explain to him in German that they are looking for a man who pulled off a bloody heist in Los Angeles, one that led to several deaths. She says if Beimler arranged the heist and is holding back information, he could be extradited to the U.S. and tried as an accomplice.

Beimler tells her he's an innocent businessman who knows nothing about robberies.

This goes on for a while.

McGrave gets more and more frustrated until finally, without any warning, he yanks Beimler out of his chair and pushes him in the river.

Maria is shocked. "What did you do that for?"

"He's lying."

"How do you know? You haven't understood a word that he's said."

"I know bullshit when I hear it," McGrave says, watching Beimler splash around in the water. "In any language."

Beimler is fighting to stay afloat. He yells, "*Hilfe! Ich kann nicht schwimmen!*"

McGrave grabs a nearby life preserver but doesn't toss it in. "Sorry, pal, me no comprendo Germano."

"I don't know how to swim!" Beimler says.

McGrave turns to Maria and smiles. "He speaks English. It's a miracle." He looks back down at Beimler. "Give me a name."

Beimler disappears under the water. Maria reaches for the life preserver, but McGrave yanks it away from her.

"He's going to drown," she says.

"I feel sorry for the fishes."

Beimler pops back up, coughing and gagging. "Richter! His name is Sebastian Richter! Now help me!"

"How do I contact him?" McGrave asks.

"I leave a message with an automated service."

"Call him, tell him you've got a job for him, and set up a meet," McGrave says. "Can you do that for me?"

"Yes!" Beimler says, but it comes out sounding more like a scream.

McGrave tosses him the life preserver, then turns to Maria. "What a helpful guy."

⌀⌀

Beimler, shivering and wet, closes his cell phone and looks across the table at McGrave and Maria, who are both nursing beers.

"Tomorrow. Midnight. The Maifeld," Beimler says. "He'll find you."

"He'd better or I'll be back," McGrave says. "I won't be so friendly next time.

McGrave and Maria get up and walk across the dock and across the beach to the car. She stops at the car and confronts him.

"You said you'd be on your best behavior."

"I was."

"You threw him in the river."

"Yes," McGrave says. "But I didn't shoot him first."

"Only because you didn't have a gun."

"I got a name and set a meet, which is a lot more than I had when I got here, so I'm a happy man."

"And if you hadn't overreacted, we could have played dumb, put Beimler under surveillance, and let him lead us to Richter. But after this stunt, and your performance at the club, everyone in Berlin knows that you're here."

"At least I get results," he says. "And it doesn't take six months undercover to do it."

☙

As glad as Maria is to be ridding herself of McGrave at his hotel, she's still a caring human being, a police officer, and someone who is proud of the city she lives in. She doesn't want to leave him here.

The two-star palace that McGrave has booked for himself on Stuttgarter is alongside greasy kebab places, cheap electronics stores, and strip clubs and has a view of the elevated S-Bahnhof, a metro rail station, where drug dealers and hookers ply their trade in the shadows under the overpass.

"Are you sure you want to stay here?" she asks.

"My travel agent highly recommends it."

"There are other hotels I can recommend in nice neighborhoods."

"I'm fine with this one," he says, and points to a sign on a lamppost. It's the McDonald's logo with an arrow underneath it that points down the street and the words "Kantstrasse at Wilmersdorf." "It's walking distance from all the major attractions."

"Suit yourself," she says. "I'll pick you up in the morning. Oh-nine-hundred hours."

"In the meantime, let's ask Hansel and Gretel back at the station to put together a file with everything you've got on Richter."

"Thanks for the suggestion, McGrave. That never would have occurred to me. Sleep well."

He gets out of the car and trudges into the hotel.

☙

The desk clerk, who looks like he combed his hair with bacon grease, then cleaned his hands with his tie, unlocks the door to McGrave's room and leads him inside.

The small room, only a little larger than the bed, is clean but has an overpowering blue motif. Blue flowered wallpaper. Blue carpet. Blue lampshades. McGrave gestures to the bed. There's a single pillow and a thick comforter, which is folded in half on the bedsheet.

"The room is fine," McGrave says. "But could you please send someone up to make the bed?"

"Make bed. Yes." The clerk speaks in heavily accented German and smiles knowingly. "I find you someone. Good price. *Mann oder Frau?*"

"No, no, I don't want anybody. The bed isn't done. I want sheets and blankets," McGrave says. The clerk stares at him blankly. So McGrave tries again. "Bedding. *Der* sheets and *der* blankets."

"The bed is here." The clerk points at it. "*Das Bett.*"

McGrave gives up and just takes the key. "Thanks, it's swell."

The clerk smiles and leaves. McGrave looks at himself in the mirror, rubs his cheeks, and frowns. It's just occurred to him that he's got no toiletries, no change of clothes, and nothing to eat.

Time to venture out into the wilderness.

∞

The market is no larger than a 7-Eleven and has only one cashier, a woman with a permanent frown, bloodshot eyes, and nicotine-stained teeth. McGrave goes up to her with a handbasket full of toiletries, a bottle of Coke, a bag of chips, and some candy bars.

She rings up his items. It's thirteen euros. He holds out a twenty to her, but she makes no move to take it. He jerks his hand towards her again. She nods at a plate on the counter in front of him. McGrave gets the message and places the cash on the plate. She scoops it up and drops some coins in its place.

McGrave pockets the money and stands there, waiting. His purchases are on the counter between them.

She looks at him.

He looks at her.

It's a long moment.

"I'm supposed to bag my own stuff?" he asks. All he gets from her is a stony look. "Okay. Fine."

He reaches for one of the plastic bags stacked nearby. She rings up .25 euro on the register.

He looks at her.

She looks at him.

He takes another bag as a test.

She rings up another .25 euro.

"You're charging me for *the bags?*" Again, she doesn't reply. She just gives him look. "The hell you are."

McGrave puts the bags back, lifts up his shirttails to create a pouch, and sweeps his stuff off the counter into it.

He smiles at her. "*Arschloch* you very much."

She flips him off.

"Lovely country," he says and walks out.

McGrave is barely out the door when he's jumped by three men, who knock him to the ground, his groceries spilling everywhere. The plastic bottle of Coke rolls down the sidewalk into the street as he struggles, to no avail. They've got him thoroughly pinned.

They quickly and expertly bind McGrave's hands and feet with duct tape, drag him to a panel van, throw him inside, and speed off.

The cashier has seen the attack but doesn't call the police. Instead, she lights a cigarette and imagines, as she often does, what it would be like to sleep with her head on German actor Til Schweiger's perfect ass.

ↄ

McGrave lies on the floor of the panel van. He is unable to

move or speak, so he keeps his eyes and ears open.

There's one guy sitting on either side of him. Both are well muscled. One is a blonde, with a square jaw, blue eyes, and a chemical tan, who probably never misses the opportunity to look at his own reflection. The other guy has a nose that resembles a clump of mashed potatoes, which means he's been in a lot of fights and doesn't know how to protect his face.

McGrave hasn't had a look at the driver yet. But the fact that Pretty Boy and Mashed Nose haven't blindfolded him means they don't care about what he sees.

Which means they aren't worried about him coming after them later.

Which means there might not be a later for him.

It doesn't take long for them to arrive at their destination, maybe fifteen minutes.

The side door slides open and the driver stands there. He's also muscled but has a blockhead that looks as if it's attached directly to his square shoulders. But No Neck's most striking feature is the huge serrated knife in his hand.

No Neck raises the knife above McGrave and brings it down for the kill.

And cuts the duct tape that binds McGrave's ankles.

The three guys all have a hearty laugh at the flash of fear that passed over McGrave's face. Then Pretty Boy and Mashed Nose lift McGrave up and push him out onto his feet.

They are parked in an abandoned industrial building, a factory of some kind, along a narrow canal off the Spree River. It's a vast space cluttered with rusting machinery and crisscrossed above with pipes and beams. The walls are brick, with hundreds of windows, most of them broken.

McGrave is led through the machinery towards Richter, who stands a few yards away, a look of smug satisfaction on his face. He is holding a gun at his side.

"Thank you, McGrave, for sparing me the effort and expense of going all the way back to LA to kill you. But you could have picked a week when I wasn't so busy. Let's make this quick. I still have lots of work to do."

Richter aims the gun at McGrave's head and Pretty Boy rips the duct tape from McGrave's mouth.

"Any last words?" Richter asks.

"You're under arrest."

Richter shares an amused look with his men and says, "*Re ist ein hirnloser kleiner Kampfhund. Geh einen Schritt zurck, ich will nicht dafl sein Hirn auf dein T-Shirt spritzt.*

The three men distance themselves from McGrave.

That's because Richer has just told them that McGrave is a mindless attack dog and that they should step back unless they want to get his brains on their shirts.

But McGrave remains surprisingly at ease for someone about to be executed.

"Keep your eyes open when you die, McGrave, and the next time I'm in LA, maybe I won't rape your daughter."

Richter is about to shoot when Maria Vogt yells from somewhere, "*Halt! Polizei!*"

The cry gives Richter a second of hesitation. McGrave uses that instant to head butt Mashed Nose in the face, breaking the thug's nose yet again, and dive for cover behind some machinery just as Richter shoots. The bullet ricochets off the machine and shatters one of the windows.

And that's when Maria, Stefan, Heinrich, and a tactical team of police officers in Kevlar spill into the warehouse, taking offensive positions behind whatever cover is available.

Pretty Boy, No Neck, and Mashed Nose take cover themselves and open fire on the cops.

Richter does the smart thing.

He runs away.

McGrave, lying helpless and angry on the ground, tries to cut his bindings on a sharp piece of metal sticking out of the old machinery.

Then he senses Pretty Boy standing over him.

McGrave rolls on his side and finds himself looking down the barrel of a gun again.

⁊

Maria is at the van now and can see what Pretty Boy intends to do.

She takes aim and fires. The bullet obliterates his right hand. It's a hell of a shot.

⁊

Pretty Boy screams in agony and clutches the stump where his hand and gun used to be.

McGrave kicks Pretty Boy's feet out from under him, and when the guy falls, kicks him in the head to shut him up.

One down.

McGrave goes back to work trying to cut the duct tape around his wrists.

⁊

The ground around the factory building is surrounded by cops.

So Richter doesn't try to flee out.

Instead, he flees up.

He effortlessly and gracefully scales the pipes and girders to the ceiling and across to the bank of windows.

The guy knows *parkour*.

⁊

Maria takes aim at Richter but can't get a clear shot at him, so she gives chase, running right past McGrave, leaving him on the ground.

She reaches the same pipes that Richter used, holsters her

weapon, and starts to climb, but for her it's far from easy.

Maria looks up.

Richter has traveled clear across the arched ceiling of the factory and is heading towards some open windows.

She climbs as quickly as she can.

ᴄⱺ

McGrave finally frees himself, sees Richter and Maria climbing, and knows there's no way he can catch up to either one of them.

So he makes a run for the way out, making himself a target for Mashed Nose and No Neck.

Mashed Nose pops up from behind the cover of machinery to take a shot at McGrave, and Stefan shoots him.

The bullet hits Mashed Nose in the chest and puts him down forever.

No Neck sees Richter above them, making his escape, and Pretty Boy with a stump where his right hand used to be, and Mashed Nose bleeding out beside him, and wisely decides that maybe single-handedly taking on a squad of heavily armed police officers isn't going to end well for him.

He tosses his gun and raises his hands in surrender.

ᴄⱺ

Richter runs along the rooftop of the factory and leaps onto an adjacent warehouse, and swings from pipe to rooftop to girder, making his way across the industrial area.

Spider-Man would be impressed.

McGrave tries to follow Richter by running alongside him on the ground, but it's futile. There are too many buildings, fences, and pipes in his way.

Richter drops onto one of a line of houseboats and floating cafés moored along the river and leapfrogs from boat to boat until he reaches a bridge, climbs up over the side, and disappears.

McGrave stops at the base of the bridge, breathing hard and pissed off.

Richter is long gone.

∽

McGrave heads back to the factory and is met halfway there by Maria.

"You moved in too soon," McGrave says, walking right past her.

She catches up, falling into step beside him. "I saved your life."

"I was doing just fine. But now, thanks to you, we've lost him."

"It wasn't until I was driving away from that shitty hotel of yours that it suddenly hit me. You wanted Richter to know you were here," Maria says. "You've been trying to attract his attention from the moment you got off the plane in that hideous shirt."

"What's wrong with my shirt?"

"The fight in the club, throwing Beimler in the river, it was all just a show."

"I don't know Berlin and I don't speak German. So obviously it's a lot easier to get him to come to me. But you've blown that."

"You dumb bastard," she says. "The only reason you're alive is because I figured out what you were doing and put you under surveillance."

"That was the plan all along."

"What *plan*? You never talked to me about any *plan*."

"It worked, didn't it? Except for the part where you let Richter get away."

"You should have told me what you were doing."

"I don't see why."

She steps in front of him, cutting him off. "Because while you're here, we're partners. And partners have to trust each other."

"Please don't call us partners," he says.

"Aren't we?"

"I hope not," he says. "My partners usually end up dead."

She cocks her head at an angle, studying him in a new light. "That may be the first real thing I've heard you say since you arrived."

"What does that mean?"

"You said something that wasn't acerbic, xenophobic, or puerile."

"I forgot to pack my thesaurus, so I have no idea what you're talking about."

"It wasn't a comment like *that*," she says. "You said something that showed some genuine concern for me and revealed a little of the sadness in you. There may actually be a caring human being behind that tough-cop act."

"Don't count on it." He steps past her and continues walking.

こ

Many of the nineteenth-century apartment blocks of Prenzlauer Berg are covered with graffiti as a design choice and painted in vibrant pastel colors, all part of the latest evolution of the neighborhood, which over the last hundred or so years has gone from working-class tenements to neglected Cold War slum to bohemian artist colony and now to a gentrified bedroom community for educated, well-off, and very horny young couples.

That horny part is fact, not snark.

More children are born in Prenzlauer Berg than anywhere else in Berlin.

That means everyone who lives here needs a car to ferry around all those kids and groceries.

And that means parking is a bitch. So if you find a spot, no matter how small, you make it work.

Maria has discovered a space between a Mercedes-Benz and an Audi and is determined to fit her car into it.

She bumps the cars in front and in back of her as she tries to parallel park between them.

"We're nowhere near my hotel, are we?" McGrave says.

"This is where I live," she says, trying to make her car fit with precise, incremental adjustments.

"What are we doing here?"

"You need a safe place to stay tonight and I need to keep an eye on you."

"So stake out my hotel."

Maria gives him a look. "Believe it or not, McGrave, I have a life."

She finally parks, her car wedged in so tight that she may not be able to get it out again without a blowtorch and the Jaws of Life.

Maria is very pleased with herself.

"No wonder they don't let you drive the BMWs," McGrave says.

⟡

They take the stairs up two flights to Maria's apartment. She unlocks the door and beckons McGrave inside, into the small living room, which is homey but overstuffed with a couch, easy chair, dining table, stacks of books, and a large TV, the kind with a picture tube, which McGrave didn't know they still made. There's a galley kitchen off the living area and a short hallway that leads to two bedrooms and a bath.

A twelve-year-old boy gets up from the couch, where he has been doing homework, and comes over to greet them. He's a gangly kid, already starting to enter that awkward phase of adolescence where his arms, legs, and neck seem to be growing at separate rates. His hair is thick and overgrown and hides his ears, but not the yellowing skin from a fading bruise around his right eye. He regards McGrave warily, and judging by how the cop looks and smells, it makes sense.

Maria closes the door and makes the introductions.

"I know it looks like I brought home a homeless guy, but this is actually a colleague, Detective John McGrave, on assignment from Los Angeles. He's been working undercover. He'll be sleeping on our couch tonight." She looks at McGrave. "This is my son, Erich."

The boy shakes McGrave's hand. "Do you know the Kardashians?"

"Who doesn't?"

"I've got some *Kohlrouladen* I can heat up," Maria says. "Set the table, Erich, and I'll bring it out in a few minutes. Make yourself at home, McGrave."

Maria and her son go into the kitchen, leaving McGrave alone. He's glancing at the books, but the titles on the spines are in German and mean nothing to him.

Erich comes out of the kitchen with the silverware and plates and starts laying it all out on the table.

"How did you get the shiner?" McGrave asks, but Erich doesn't get it. "Your swollen eye."

"Axel Sand."

"Is this the first time he's given you one of those?

Erich shakes his head sadly. "He's older, bigger, and tougher than I am."

"Then he'll never know what hit him." McGrave waves Erich away from the table. "Let me show you a couple of tricks."

℗

Maria is grating horseradish and is about to tend to the boiled potatoes when she hears a grunt and crash from the living room. She rushes out into the living room to see the coffee table tipped over and McGrave facedown on the floor, Erich standing over him, his foot firmly planted between McGrave's shoulder blades, and twisting the cop's arm behind his back.

Erich is grinning. So is McGrave.

"McGrave calls this the crippler," Erich says.

"How nice," Maria says. "The *Kohlrouladen* is ready. I've boiled some potatoes, too."

Erich releases McGrave, who sits up and says, "What's kohl-roo-what's-it?"

"Cabbage stuffed with minced meat."

"Yum," he says. "Are there any Pizza Huts nearby?"

೮೨

It's after dinner. The dirty dishes and the Pizza Hut box are still on the table. Erich has gone to bed. McGrave is sitting on the couch, having a Coke, which he drinks out of the bottle. Maria brings out some bedding and some men's clothes and sets them on the coffee table.

"I'm sorry you didn't like dinner."

"I loved it."

"I meant the *Kohlrouladen*," she says.

"I'm not big on foreign foods."

"Your pizza was made here with local ingredients."

"But it tastes just like home," he says.

She motions to the clothes. "Those are clean clothes. They should be about your size. You can keep them."

"Isn't your husband going to miss them?"

"If he did, he would have picked them up months ago," she says. "We're divorcing."

"Any particular reason why?"

She sits down next to him and sighs. "Over the years, we became very different people. I became a police detective and Karl became a homeopathic doctor."

McGrave snorts. "You mean he tells people they'll get better if they eat herbs and roots and stuff."

"More or less."

"So he's not a doctor," McGrave says. "He's a salad chef."

Maria tries to stifle a smile and fails. McGrave smiles, too.

"So where does the kid fit into this?" he asks.

"In the middle, unfortunately. My ex-husband and I are fighting for custody. Karl says my job 'creates an unstable and violent living environment that's unsuitable for raising children.'"

McGrave nods. "I didn't fight my ex for custody of my daughter.

I knew Maddie would be better off with her. And I was right."

"How old is your daughter?"

"Seventeen." McGrave reaches into his pocket, pulls out his wallet, and shows her a picture.

"She's beautiful," Maria says. "What's the real reason you chased Richter all the way over here?"

"It's my job."

She shakes her head. "Try again."

"He threatened to kill my family," he says. "And the bastard executed my bulldog."

"Richter killed your dog?"

"He was my partner, too."

McGrave's wallet is still open in his hand. Maria tugs out the photo that's behind the one of his daughter. It's a creased, yellowed picture of McGrave when he was a young uniformed officer astride his police-issue Harley-Davidson.

"What's this?"

"A picture from my days as a patrolman before I made detective. Sometimes I really miss them," he says. "How about you?"

"Miss what?"

"Don't you ever wish you were back in uniform again, rolling on calls, working the streets?"

"I was never a patrol officer."

McGrave stares at her in disbelief. "Then how did you become a detective?"

"The usual way," she says. "I studied for two years at the Akademie für Verwaltung und Rechtspflege and was hired as a *Kriminalkommissar* upon graduation."

She gets up and starts clearing the dishes from the table. McGrave gets up and helps her.

"You didn't spend any time in uniform?"

"In Germany, the uniformed officers, the *Schutzpolizei*, are a separate force from the investigators, the *Kriminalpolizei*. You don't serve as a *Schutzpolizei* in order to become a *Kriminalpolizei*."

McGrave can't believe what he is hearing. "So everything you know about being a cop you've learned from *books*?"

"Of course. That's how it's done." She takes the dishes into the kitchen.

McGrave follows her. "No, it's not. You can't develop instincts from a book. You've got to be out there, on the streets, living it."

"That's ridiculous," she says, taking the dishes from him and putting them in the sink. "Officers prevent crimes and protect people from danger. Detectives investigate crimes and pursue the offenders. They are two entirely different skills. A detective must be highly educated."

"Where I come from," he says, "the university is *the street*."

"Where I come from," she says, "the university is *a university*."

"That explains a lot about the police work I've seen from you today," McGrave says.

He regrets the remark almost the instant he's said it, but it's too late.

"Likewise," she says. "Good night, Detective."

She leaves the dishes in the sink and marches off to bed.

∽

The squad room is busy. Maria is at her desk, reviewing a file. Stefan is working the phones. Heinrich is doing something on his computer and eating chocolate somethings from a yellow bag with a picture of what looks like five pieces of horse crap on the front.

McGrave strides in wearing the too-small shirt that Maria gave him under his leather jacket. The pants are a little tight, too. He's holding a huge box of Dunkin' Donuts.

"Look what I found. Some real cop brain food." He sets the box down in front of Heinrich and opens it up to reveal dozens of mixed doughnuts as if they were gold bars. "Feast on this, my friends, and you shall solve all the world's crimes."

"No, thank you," Heinrich says. "But you are welcome to one of these."

He offers McGrave the open bag of Zetti Knusperflocken

Vollmilch Schokolade mit Knäckebrot.

McGrave peers inside the bag and shakes his head. "What is it?"

"*Knusperflocken*. One of the few treats left from the GDR. I have to order it on the Internet now."

"You lived there before the wall fell?"

"I was a *Volkspolizist*. Duke was, too. In the East, it was different. The people didn't dare break the law. The police were respected and feared. Here there is much lawlessness and they spit on our shoes."

"Do you miss it?"

"No, the police should not be feared. But I miss the strict adherence to the law. And the food was better."

McGrave takes a doughnut. Heinrich has another piece of *Knusperflocken*.

Neither of them is ever going to change.

"What have you got on Richter?" McGrave asks.

"He goes all over the world staging major heists and doesn't mind killing. He was reportedly trained by the *Bundesnachrichtendienst*."

"What's the Bundy-what's-it?" McGrave asks.

"Our CIA," Heinrich says. "That explains why he's never been caught. Richter probably still does a few jobs for them, so in return they make sure he doesn't show up in the system."

"Richter said he's prepping a job right now," McGrave says.

Stefan hangs up the phone. "That fits with what the detectives in the robbery division just told me. There's rumors floating around that somebody is looking for alarm specialists, tunnelers, and a wheelman for a big job."

"Are Richter's two gun monkeys saying anything?" McGrave asks.

"Not a word," Stefan says.

That's when Maria comes over. "They don't have to. Their shoes are talking for them."

"Their shoes," McGrave says.

"I had the forensics unit analyze their clothing and the van they used to abduct you," she says. "A soils analysis of the dirt particles found on their shoes and the undercarriage of the van points to one place."

"Which is?" McGrave asks.

❧

Maria and McGrave stand on a mound of excavated dirt in a vacant lot in the Mitte, formerly the administrative center of the Third Reich and, after the war, the GDR, too. The office space was, after all, already designed to meet the needs of those engaged in the hard work of censorship and oppression.

Today there are construction cranes everywhere, and big, elevated blue pipes snake along the side streets and major boulevards.

"Ever since reunification, there's been a construction boom in Mitte," Maria explains. "The wastelands and abandoned buildings left behind when the wall fell became prime real estate for development and renovation. I think it's finally coming to an end. Thank God."

The blockish, symmetrical buildings are nearly flush with one another and were designed to reflect Hitler's "Words of Stone" monumental style, espousing a message of rigid order, intimidating power, and enforced conformity.

They still do, only now they're adorned with polished stone and glass and buffed to a Disney gleam, and they proclaim the enduring and awesome power of money, the virtues of accumulating wealth, and the importance of spending what you have on the priciest material goods you can afford.

"What are those elevated blue pipes I see everywhere?" McGrave asks.

"They move the groundwater from the construction sites to the river," she says. "It's the unique nature of that sediment that allowed us to trace the dirt in Richter's van back here."

McGrave looks around him, trying to get his bearings. But it's not easy.

All the buildings are the same height and shape and topped by three terraced stories, creating an unbroken roofline down every street, so they appear to be part of an immense wall, broken only by the side streets.

It's almost like McGrave is standing in the center of an immense labyrinth.

And within that labyrinth, there are scores of galleries, jewelry stores, banks, and museums. There's even a billboard by the construction site advertising an exhibition in Mitte of Fabergé eggs.

Any one of those places could be Richter's next target.

Maria's cell phone rings. She answers it, says something in German, then turns to McGrave.

"Excuse me," she says. "I need to take this."

She steps aside, out of earshot. But a breeze kicks up and McGrave's attention is suddenly drawn to something else a half block away.

He heads across the street, weaving through the traffic and across iron plates laid over trenches cut into the asphalt, and on past several storefronts, until he reaches a gallery with a large, banner draped across the top four floors. He'd caught a glimpse of it fluttering in the breeze.

The banner is in German, but it depicts glassware and ceramics, including the item that attracted McGrave—a pot that looks just like the one destroyed in the shoot-out in Ernie Wallengren's house.

Maria marches up to him. She seems angry. "Looking for some souvenirs?"

"Tell me what the banner says."

"It's advertising an auction of rare Egyptian antiquities. The auction is tomorrow, but you're going to be—"

"On a plane back to Los Angeles with Richter handcuffed beside me," McGrave says, interrupting her and pointing at the banner. "Because that son of a bitch is going to try to steal Nefertiti's toilet tonight and I'm going to be there to catch him."

⌘

Torsten "Duke" Schneider and Maria stand side by side in front of a full house of detectives, briefing them in English, out of deference to McGrave, on the operation that they've hurriedly put into motion.

On the wall behind Torsten and Maria is a street map of Mitte as well as photographs of the interior and exterior of the auction house, schematic diagrams of sewers, and other blueprints.

"We believe that Richter and his new team will strike the auction house tonight and use the World War Two–era tunnels beneath Wilhelmstrasse to do it," Maria says. "The construction work in the area provided the perfect cover for him to access the tunnels and dig his way beneath the auction house without raising any suspicion."

Torsten uses a pointer to indicate spots on the street map.

"Two-man surveillance teams will be placed here, here, and here," he says, pointing to buildings facing the front and rear of the auction house. "We've also placed fiber-optic cameras into the tunnels and will monitor them in our mobile command unit, which will be parked here." He points to the lot where Maria and McGrave stood earlier. "Our strike unit will be stationed in an empty, unoccupied storefront around the corner from the auction house. They will move in on my signal. I want everyone in place within the hour. You each have your assignments. Let's get moving."

The detectives disperse. Torsten and Maria approach McGrave, who is sitting at Maria's desk.

Torsten helps himself to a frosted chocolate doughnut with chocolate sprinkles from the box on Heinrich's desk.

"These doughnuts really energize your thinking," Torsten says. "I can see why they are so popular among law enforcement officers in the U.S. This is my third one today."

"I didn't get an assignment," McGrave says.

"You'll be observing from the command post."

McGrave shakes his head. "I don't observe, Duke, I act. I need to lead the strike team."

"I'm afraid I can't allow it," Torsten says. "You don't have any jurisdiction and you can't carry a weapon."

"This is all the jurisdiction I need," McGrave holds up his badge. "And I'm a weapon."

Maria groans.

Torsten beams. "Say it again."

"What?" McGrave says.

"'I'm a weapon.' It's so . . . so . . ."

"John Wayne," Maria says.

"Exactly!" Torsten says.

"So I can be on the team?"

"Absolutely not," Torsten says. "But you will be welcome in the trailer. I'll even provide doughnuts. You're with Kommissar Vogt until then."

Her cell phone rings. She glances at the caller ID. It's Erich's school.

☙

Like much of the architecture of the GDR era, the *Oberschule* looks like a concrete shoe box that's been spray painted with graffiti.

School has been dismissed and there are only a few kids hanging around.

Maria and McGrave emerge from the Passat to find Erich sitting on a concrete bench out front. Erich is sitting with a man who is roughly McGrave's height and build, but that's where the similarities end.

You look at him and see a guy who reads avant-garde novels, not because he likes them, but so he can say he reads avant-garde novels. You look at him and you see a closet full of sweaters and scarves, because he lives in a perpetual winter, needs to be swaddled all the time, and likes having clothes to shed at coffeehouses, where he spends more time than in his own home. You look at him and see a lover who gets tears in his eyes when he makes love because otherwise it would be fucking and because no matter how many times he does it, he's always afraid it will never happen again.

"This is my ex-husband, Karl," Maria says, then gestures to McGrave. "This is John McGrave, a detective from America."

"Isn't that *my* shirt?" Karl says.

Maria ignores him and turns to Erich. "What happened? All they told me was that you were in a fight with another boy."

Karl speaks up before his son can. "It was a shocking act of violence and depravity."

McGrave glances at Erich. There isn't a scratch or bruise on him. "He looks like he came out okay."

"He's been expelled for a week," Karl says. "That is hardly 'okay.'"

McGrave nods. "What's Axel look like?"

Erich breaks into a big, proud grin, but before he can speak, Karl answers for him again. "Erich broke the boy's arm."

Maria gasps.

McGrave smiles, which is all the encouragement Erich needs.

"It was great," Erich says in an excited rush, eager to share the experience. "He swung at me and I took him completely by surprise, just like you showed me."

Karl glowers at Maria. "Congratulations, you've turned our son into a sociopath."

Maria isn't any happier about this than Karl is. She turns to McGrave and crosses her arms under her chest, mostly so she won't be tempted to hit him.

"You taught Erich how to break someone's arm?"

"I showed him how to defend himself," McGrave says, and glances at Karl. "It's about time somebody did."

Karl shakes his head and looks at Maria. "What were you thinking, bringing this caveman into your bed?"

"I'm not sleeping with him," Maria says.

"He's just wearing my clothes and teaching my son how to kill," Karl says. "I'm sure the judge will find your promiscuity and choice of men very interesting. I just hope it's not too late to save my son."

"Oh, stop being so melodramatic," Maria says.

Karl gives his son a hug and stands up. "I will see you soon. Be strong."

"He is now," McGrave says. "No thanks to you."

"Shut up, McGrave," Maria says.

Karl walks away. Maria turns to Erich.

"Stay here." She pulls McGrave aside, out of Erich's earshot, and then lays into him. "Do you realize what you've done?"

"You don't have to thank me. Just seeing the confidence and pride on Erich's face is enough."

"You may have just cost me custody of my son," Maria said.

"Erich was being bullied by Axel for weeks. Axel had this coming. You should be happy your son defended himself."

"I'll tell you what's going to make me happy," she says. "Putting you on the next flight to Los Angeles. It leaves in two hours, and you're on it."

"Not without Richter," McGrave says.

"Yes, you are. I know all about you, Tidal Wave. I talked to your captain today."

McGrave winces. "That was the call you got in Mitte this afternoon. You needed privacy because you were speaking in English and didn't want me to hear you."

"That's right. I know you're not a cop anymore. You're a fraud."

"If you knew, why didn't you say anything to Duke?"

"Because I'm a fool. I was going to let you stay one more night to see Richter get caught."

"You still can," McGrave says.

"Not now, not after this," she says. "I'm taking you to the airport or I am taking you to jail. It's up to you."

McGrave is fucked.

⟡

It's almost nightfall. Torsten and Heinrich are in the same panel van that was parked outside of Der Reizvolle. The images on the two monitors are divided into quarters so the detectives can simultaneously watch views of the street, the tunnels, and several angles on the auction house.

"It smells disgusting in here," Torsten says.

"The surveillance went on for weeks and this is a tiny space," Heinrich says apologetically. "And we had a little accident with the Porta-Potty."

"What kind of accident?"

"It might have spilled."

"It might have or it did?"

Before Heinrich can answer, a report comes in over the radio from one of the observers.

"This is Unit Two. We've got something. The construction site on the northeast corner."

Torsten taps Heinrich on the shoulder. "Show me."

Heinrich hits a button and a feed comes up full screen on one of the monitors.

What they see is an enormous pit that has been excavated and reinforced for what will be an office building's foundation and underground garage.

The construction site is closed.

A van drives up to the locked gate.

A man dressed in black, his back to the camera, gets out of the van with a pair of bolt cutters and snaps the chain securing the gate. He holds the gate open and the van drives in, parking under one of the big, blue elevated water pipes that snakes out from the site, across the street, and down to the Spree.

Four men dressed in black, wearing balaclavas over their heads and carrying large gym bags, get out of the van and make their way down into the enormous pit.

Torsten picks up the mike. "Attention, all units. The robbery is in progress. Hold your positions." He turns to Heinrich. "Where are Vogt and McGrave?"

❧

They are in Maria's Passat on a busy boulevard, headed towards Berlin-Tegel Airport. Maria is driving, resolute in her mission. McGrave sits beside her, pissed off but helpless. Erich is in the backseat, sitting in the middle so he can see them both.

"You can't make him go, Mom," Erich says.

"Watch me," she says.

"But I broke Axel's arm, not McGrave. Send me to America," Erich says. "Disney World, for instance."

Her cell phone rings. She answers it and begins carrying on a conversation in German. McGrave's name is mentioned. He looks over his shoulder at Erich.

"What's she saying?" McGrave asks.

"She's says you can't participate in the operation. Something urgent came up."

"What could be more urgent than catching Richter?"

Erich listens to his mother talk, then: "She says you have food poisoning. You can't stop vomiting."

Maria ends the call and wedges her phone into the ashtray. McGrave looks at her.

"It's happening, isn't it?" he says.

"You were right, McGrave. It's tonight. Richter has walked into a trap and he doesn't even know it. We got lucky."

"And I'm missing it," McGrave says.

"We'll send you a postcard."

※

On a rooftop in Mitte, a cop wearing a headphone mike aims a camera at the auction house across the street. It's the kind of camera that picks up heat signatures.

Torsten's voice comes through the cop's earpiece. "Are they inside?"

The cop looks at the tiny screen on the camera and sees an X-ray-like image of the auction house and the distinct red silhouettes of four men climbing up through the floor.

"They're in," the cop says.

૮૭

Heinrich is on his hands and knees in the van, scrubbing the floor with a rag and cleanser. Torsten is at the console, leaning into the mike.

"All units, hold your positions. No one moves until I say so."

૮૭

Maria and McGrave aren't moving, either. Their car is stuck in traffic, right beside a billboard advertising the Fabergé egg exhibit.

Which is in Mitte.

Where all the action is happening.

Without him.

It's salt in the wound.

Actually, it's more like ground glass, battery acid, and gasoline in the wound.

McGrave drums his fingers on the armrest.

Maria looks at him. "Would you please stop that?"

"I was lost here. I've never been to Berlin and I don't speak German. But I outflanked Richter anyway."

"You had a little help," she says.

"You're right, I did. You picked up rumors about someone looking for tunnelers and alarm pros. You found unique dirt particles that led us to a specific neighborhood. And I stumbled on an auction of Egyptian toilets, just like the ones Richter was trying to steal in LA."

"Toilets?" Erich says, a note of disappointment in his voice. "You're chasing a guy who steals toilets? What kind of supercriminal is that?"

"It all fell together so easily," McGrave says.

Maria shrugs. "Sometimes it does."

"It *never* does," he says.

"It does when you work with a skilled team, in a precise and thoughtful manner, rather than charging into the streets on your own. You hate that you needed help."

"That's not it."

"And now you're furious because Richter is going to be arrested in the middle of his robbery and you'll be somewhere over the Atlantic when it happens."

"I'm not going to be there," he says. He looks out the window again at the billboard.

"That's right," Maria says, as if reprimanding a child. "I hope you've learned a lesson from this."

"You see that egg?" He gestures to the billboard. "Where is that exhibit?"

"It's in a private museum created to show off the art collection of Matthias Balz, the international real estate tycoon," she says. "It's in a renovated air-raid bunker built by the Nazis to evacuate travelers from Friedrichstrasse train station."

"Where's that in relation to the robbery that's going down?"

"A few blocks away," she says.

McGrave sits up straight in his seat. "And we aren't there."

"Stop whining, McGrave," she says. "It's childish."

"What I'm saying is that we aren't *there*." McGrave points to the billboard. "That's where Richter really is, stealing the Fabergé eggs and God knows what else. We were set up."

"Oh really?" she says. "Then who is robbing the auction house right now?"

"Whoever they are, they have been set up by Richter, too. It's all a distraction from the *real* robbery."

Maria shakes her head. "You're reaching. You're just desperate to stay off that plane."

"Maybe I am. But what if I'm right? You have nothing to lose by checking it out," he says. "If I am wrong, I promise I will take the next flight."

"You're like a child who doesn't want to go to bed."

"You have to help him, Mom," Erich says.

"Why should I?" Maria says. "Thanks to him, you're expelled and the judge is going to say I'm responsible for it. I could lose you."

"You'll never lose me."

Maria looks in her rearview mirror at her son. He looks right back at her.

"He helped me, Mom, even if you don't think so," Erich says. "You may not owe him anything, but I do."

Maria knows she's going to regret this, but . . .

"Don't ever tell your dad about this."

She makes a sharp U-turn over the grassy median and veers across the path of oncoming traffic, causing a dozen cars to come to a screeching, rubber-ripping stop to avoid collisions.

And then she floors it, weaving around the cars ahead and speeding towards the center of Berlin.

Erich lets out a cheer.

Maria has just become the coolest mother *ever*.

છ

The Fabergé Egg

From *Wikipedia*, the free encyclopedia (and because it's compiled, fact-checked, and updated strictly by anybody with an Internet connection, it is the most detailed and reliable source of all human knowledge)

A Fabergé egg (Russian: Яйца Фаберже; Yaĭtsa Faberzhe) is any one of the thousands of jeweled eggs made by the House of Fabergé from 1885 to 1917. The most famous eggs were the larger ones made for Alexander III and Nicholas II of Russia; these are often referred to as the "Imperial" Fabergé eggs. Of the fifty made, forty-two have survived. All of the eggs are made of precious metals or hard stones decorated with enamel and gems. The Fabergé eggs have become the ultimate symbol of luxury and are considered masterpieces.

છ

Stefan leads the elite assault team that is standing around in an empty storefront in their heavy assault gear with their assault weapons, all anxiously waiting for the go-ahead to assault.

Torsten's voice suddenly crackles in Stefan's earpiece.

"The robbers are leaving the auction house. Take position around the construction site and be ready to apprehend them as they emerge from the pit."

Stefan takes out his badge and drapes it on a chain around his neck, McGrave-style, so it hangs over his Kevlar vest.

He looks cool and he knows it. If only there was someone around to take a picture.

Stefan alerts his team with a few tactical hand signals, which he's been practicing with his girlfriend for months while shopping at the enormous and crowded KaDeWe, and they move out the door with professional resolve and military precision.

⁋

The five-story air-raid bunker that houses the Balz Collection is a monstrous symmetrical block of exposed reinforced concrete, its six-foot-thick walls and narrow window slits still showing the pockmarks and chips left by bullets and artillery fire during World War II.

It was later used by the GDR as a massive storage bin for imported Cuban fruits and vegetables set aside for the consumption of the government elite. After the Berlin Wall fell, the fortress-like bunker became an enormous, and extremely hard-core, techno-fetish club, which is how Matthias Balz discovered it (and a lasting appreciation for the erotic possibilities of neoprene).

It wasn't until the early 2000s, after the club had died, that Balz bought the empty bunker and renovated it at a cost of millions to expose his fabulous art collection, by appointment only, to select members of the public.

But he isn't the only one who has bought up neglected architectural relics of the Third Reich and dumped enormous amounts of money into them for renovation. The entire city block is under construction. Huge cranes loom all around the bunker and the neighboring buildings. Those elevated blue water pipes are everywhere.

Maria drives up and easily finds a parking spot behind a tiny yellow Smart Fortwo, which looks like a car made for Smurfs.

She turns to Erich in the backseat. "Stay in the car with the doors locked, no matter what happens. If there's trouble, call the police on your cell phone."

Erich nods, a big grin on his face. Life has become a lot more exciting since McGrave showed up.

Maria and McGrave get out of the car and cross the empty street towards the bunker. It's a stark, cold, imposing structure, designed to convey the invincibility of the Third Reich.

The street is empty.

No traffic.

No people.

No sound.

It's about as lifeless as a movie studio back lot.

"Face it, McGrave," Maria says. "You're wrong."

❧

Stefan and his team are in position at the construction site around the edge of the pit, their weapons aimed into it, waiting for the robbers to emerge from the tunnels below.

There's no way Richter and the robbers can escape. They are surrounded from above and there's another assault team coming up behind them in the tunnel from the auction house.

It's basically over. The robbers just don't know it yet.

So for Torsten, Heinrich, Stefan, and all the other cops involved, it's anticlimactic.

Everyone's attention is on the pit. No one is paying any attention to the van that the robbers arrived in.

And why should they?

Nobody is inside it.
They looked.
But they didn't look underneath it.
If they did, they would have seen the bomb.

⌘

The van explodes, obliterating the water pipe above it.

⌘

From where Maria and McGrave are standing, they can feel the rumble from the blast and see the flash in the night sky several blocks away.
"It's showtime," McGrave says.

⌘

The force of the explosion and the blast of water from the severed pipe sweep the assault team off their feet, hurling several of them into the pit.

⌘

Bombs explode under key portions of the elevated water pipes throughout Mitte, one after the other, releasing torrents of water onto the streets, mowing over people, and snarling traffic.

⌘

Maria and McGrave can hear the pandemonium: the honking horns, the sirens, and the countless alarms set off by the percussion of the blast. Water rolls down the street towards them. They look at each other, then at the bunker, just as its alarm goes off.
"Okay, you were right, I was wrong." She takes out her cell

phone.

"What are you doing?"

"Calling for backup."

"They'll never get here in time," he says. "The streets are going to be gridlocked."

"Then how is Richter going to get away?"

McGrave looks up. So does she, just in time to see Richter atop the bunker, wearing a backpack. He leaps onto a line dangling from a construction crane and swings to the next rooftop.

Spider-Man, eat your heart out.

"Not again," McGrave says, and looks at the Smart Fortwo parked beside him.

୧୬

The Smart Fortwo is the midget offspring of a drunken, corporate one-night stand between Swatch, maker of rubber watches, and Mercedes-Benz, maker of fine automobiles. Swatch ran off in the morning and left Mercedes to raise the Fortwo, which measures a mere eight feet long and five feet wide, about the same as a typical golf cart. The Fortwo is propelled by a three-cylinder, seventy-one-horsepower, rear-mounted engine that is about as powerful as a decent outboard motor or the combined force of twenty-three elderly women in their motorized chairs.

McGrave takes a step back, lifts his right leg, and sticks his foot through the driver's-side window of the car, smashing out the glass. He opens the door, sweeps away the glass from the seat with his jacket, and squeezes inside.

୧୬

Maria takes out her gun and shoots at Richter, who eludes her, fleeing across the rooftops using his amazing *parkour* skills.

McGrave yanks some wires from under the dash, starts the car, and pulls out of the parking space, nearly hitting Maria.

"What are you doing?" she says.

"Giving chase," he says. "Are you coming or not?"

She points to Erich. "Stay here."

Maria hops in the car and McGrave speeds off.

∾

McGrave races their car down the empty street, peering up at the buildings as he steers to follow Richter's progress jumping from rooftop to rooftop.

"I'll watch," Maria says. "You drive."

McGrave heads onto a busy boulevard, which is full of water and clogged with cars, so he drives up onto the sidewalk, forcing people to leap out of his way and slip on the slick concrete.

"Where is he?"

"Keep going straight," she says. "Where did you learn how to steal a car?"

"My university," he says. "Didn't they teach you how in yours?"

"Left!" she says.

McGrave makes a sharp turn at the next street, but this one isn't just gridlocked with cars. The sidewalks are also gone, removed to make room for the blue pipes, which are now spewing water.

There's nowhere for him to drive.

He looks up at the rooftops. He is losing sight of Richter in the distance.

"We're not going to catch him like this," McGrave says. "He's going somewhere. But where? If you couldn't use the streets, how would you escape?"

Maria thinks a moment. "The Spree-Kanal. That's where he's heading. It feeds into the river. If he's got a boat, he can disappear in minutes."

"Which way is it?"

"West," she says.

McGrave turns the wheel to his right and floors it, driving through the glass doors of an office building.

"I didn't mean that literally," Maria says.

"We don't have a lot of choices," he says.

McGrave drives the tiny car across the lobby, past the elevators, and through the glass doors on the other side.

☙

The car bursts onto the next block, but the street is also clogged with traffic, so he makes a hard left onto the sidewalk, driving until he spots a narrow opening between cars.

He makes a right turn, squeezing between two cars and shearing off his mirrors, and charges into a courtyard on the opposite side of the street.

The courtyard is full of outdoor cafés, shops, and artists selling their wares at tiny kiosks. People sit at tables and stroll along the narrow, twisting passageways that give the place an Old World charm.

Or at least they *did*.

Now they are scrambling out of McGrave's path as he honks his horn and mows through tables, merchandise, and artwork on his path through the passageways.

They blast out of the courtyard and onto a small plaza ringed with buildings.

It's a dead end.

He comes to a screeching stop.

They are facing a modern office building. It's two stories tall, all glass. Two escalators, with a staircase between them, connect the lobby to the second floor.

"We have to turn around," Maria says.

"The hell I will."

McGrave heads right for the lobby.

☙

McGrave smashes through the glass and drives up onto the

escalators, the car straddling the staircase in between, the tires using the wide handrails as a ramp to the second floor.

He stops the car on the landing, not quite sure where to go next.

Workers are coming out of their offices and cubicles to gape at this unbelievable sight.

All the color has drained out of Maria's face. She has never been more terrified in her life.

Or more thrilled.

"Are you completely insane?" she says.

"Not yet," he says, steering the car down the hallway until he finds a window with a westerly view. "But I'm getting there."

From where the tiny car is parked, McGrave and Maria can see the rooftops of the nearby buildings.

And they can see Richter, going from building to building with grace and ease, seemingly without a care in the world.

They are ahead of him, just above the warehouse rooftop that stands between Richter and the Spree-Kanal, where a speedboat is moored.

Maria can see what McGrave is thinking.

"Don't even think about it," she says.

"You're right," he says.

She relaxes into her seat. "Thank God."

"It's better to just do it."

He backs up, shifts into drive, and floors it.

⌘

The car bursts out of the building in a spray of plaster and glass and flies across the street onto the rooftop of the next building at almost the same instant that Richter lands there . . .

⌘

The car hits the rooftop and slides to a stop right in front of

Richter, who is totally shocked.

Maria throws open her door and aims her gun at him.

"Halt! Polizei! Du bist unter Anhalten."

She's a little dazed, and dizzy, and her hands are shaking, but Richter is still dead in her sights and he knows it.

Richter raises his hands, beaten.

McGrave smiles at Maria. "Book 'em, Danno."

❧

Richter is handcuffed to the wrecked Smart Fortwo and is seething with rage. He's wishing now that he'd let Maria shoot him rather than endure this humiliation.

McGrave and Maria stand together at the edge of the roof. He's looking out at the Spree. She's holding Richter's backpack and examining the Fabergé eggs inside.

"What are you going to tell Duke?" McGrave asks.

She zips up the backpack and slings it over her shoulder. "That you're a suicidal lunatic who shouldn't be allowed anywhere near a car."

"And?"

She smiles at him. "It's a good thing you're a cop in Los Angeles and not here. Just be sure you're on a plane tomorrow."

"I can't wait to leave," he says.

That's when Torsten, Stefan, and Heinrich come through the rooftop door. The three of them are all wearing their badges on chains around their necks. Stefan is soaked and muddy. They all stop and gape at the wrecked car.

Torsten looks from the wrecked car on the roof to the broken window in the next building, then back again. He's clearly imagining the jump.

Holy crap.

"Now, that's determination," Torsten says.

"That's one word for it, sir," Maria says. "I can think of a few others."

"Two major robberies were thwarted in one night and all the criminals involved are in custody," Torsten says. "It doesn't get any better than that in our business."

"Except Berlin will have to begin the reconstruction all over again," she says.

Stefan and Heinrich are taking pictures with their cell phones of the car and Richter, who is cursing them in German.

Torsten shifts his gaze to McGrave. "Are all the cops in America like you?"

"No," McGrave says. "But they should be."

❧

For the last twenty years, the most popular show on German television has been *Alarm für Cobra 11*. It's about two detectives with the *Autobahnpolizei* who, naturally, take on drug cartels, kidnappers, international assassins, bank robbers, and nuclear terrorists while destroying as many cars, motorcycles, buses, motor homes, eighteen-wheelers, and gasoline tankers as they possibly can along the way. (Because we all know that's what cops on the highway do, as opposed to, say, giving people tickets for speeding, taking recliners out of lanes, and responding to accidents). It's not uncommon to see fifty cars, a helicopter, a boat, a train, and half of downtown Düsseldorf obliterated in just the opening scene of a typical episode.

So it should come as no surprise that the German authorities took McGrave's pursuit of Sebastian Richter in stride.

In fact, they got McGrave a room for the night at the Hyatt at Potsdammer Platz and even bought him a fresh set of clothes and toiletries.

So when Maria Vogt sees John McGrave now, walking around a bright yellow, two-door Trabant with Kriminalhauptkommissar Torsten Schneider in the police station parking lot, it's the first time he's appeared clean and rested since they met.

A car chase through city streets, especially one that leads to an arrest, always leaves McGrave feeling pretty good.

Maria is carrying a box with a ribbon on it, a gift for McGrave. It's the least she can do. Now that he's leaving, it feels as if he's taking all of the stress in her life away on the plane with him.

And not just the troubles he's caused her, either. But *everything*. Somehow, nothing seems too big to handle after what she survived last night. The terrifying experience put everything in her life into perspective. It has even changed Erich. This morning, for the first time in ages, he was looking forward to going to school.

As she walks across the parking lot, Torsten and McGrave are finishing their initial inspection of the mint-condition vintage Trabant, a car that wasn't made with sheet metal, but rather Duroplast, a mixture of plastic and cotton that is noncorrosive but that provides about as much safety to an occupant in an accident as you would have if you wrapped yourself in aluminum foil before jumping in front of a speeding train.

"It was the official car of the GDR," Torsten explains to McGrave. "I was on a waiting list for sixteen years to get this. The day after it arrived, the Berlin Wall fell and I could have had any car I wanted."

"How does it drive, Duke?" McGrave asks.

"It's probably the worst car ever made," Torsten says, "but I can't bring myself to let go of it."

"It's hard to let go of your dreams, especially when they come true."

"What was yours?" Torsten asks.

"To be a cop," McGrave replies just as Maria joins them, holding her box.

"Don't let him drive your car, sir," she says to Torsten. "Trust me on this."

McGrave gestures to the box. "What have you got there?"

"A gift for you," she says. "I'll hold it while you open it."

It seems like an odd request, but he complies, untying the ribbon and lifting off the top.

A bulldog puppy launches itself like a jack-in-the-box into

McGrave's arms and starts enthusiastically licking his face.

McGrave holds the dog up in front of him to get a good look at his face and then grins with delight. He is clearly touched.

"I don't know what to say, Maria."

"Good-bye is enough," she says. "Now you have a partner again."

"Two," Torsten says.

"*Two?*" Maria says.

McGrave lets the dog lick his face some more. "Duke just gave us another case."

"*Us?*" Maria says.

"I have good news for you," Torsten says. "Detective McGrave has agreed to become a special consultant to the *Schwerstkriminalitat.*"

McGrave holds the dog with one hand and flashes his *Kommissar* badge at her with the other. "Nice, isn't it? Comes with a leather carrying case, too."

"You two will be working together," Torsten says.

"Sir, he can't stay," she says.

"I've arranged everything with the government," he says. "It's done."

Maria glares at McGrave, who is petting his new puppy. "Sorry, McGrave, but you've given me no choice." She looks back at her boss. "He should have told you this himself. He's not a cop. He was fired from the LAPD before he came here."

Torsten waves off her concern. "I know that."

"You do?" she says.

"I've known it from the moment he arrived," he says. "But I've always wanted to work with an American cop. The LAPD's loss is our gain."

"Only until I can settle my legal problems back home," McGrave says, "and not a moment longer."

Maria ignores him. "Sir, do you know what they call him there? *Tidal Wave McGrave.* Do you know why? Just look at what he did last night. He stole a car, smashed through two buildings, and caused hundreds of thousands of euros in damages."

"Thank you for reminding me about damages," Torsten says. "I'd almost forgotten."

"I'm glad you're seeing reason, sir."

"I noticed some dents on the front and rear bumpers of your official car, Frau Kommissar," Torsten says. "When are you going to learn how to park? The cost of those repairs will be coming out of your paycheck."

She stares at him. "You can't be serious, sir."

"Duke is right, Maria," McGrave says. "You really have to be more responsible."

"*You're* telling *me* that?" she says.

"Watch and learn," McGrave says and walks away with his puppy.

This should be fun.

AUTHOR'S NOTE AND ACKNOWLEDGMENTS

I've taken a few outrageous geographical liberties with Berlin, a city I dearly love and where I lived while researching, writing, and producing *Fast Track*, an action movie that was set there. It's been a few years since then, so the city as depicted in this story reflects my fond memories much more than it does the reality of Berlin today.

I could not, and would not, have written this novella, which began as a television pilot, if not for the encouragement, enthusiasm, and support of my good friend Hermann Joha, who introduced Germany to me and was responsible for two of the most fun and exciting years of my career.

I am also indebted to Elke Schubert, Daniel Hetzer, Alexander Schust, Heiko Schmidt, Axel Sand, Fran McConnell, Gavin Reardon, Stefan Retzbach, Kay Niessen, Katrina Wood, and Mitchel Stein for their invaluable contributions to this work.

—Lee Goldberg

OTHER BOOKS BY LEE GOLDBERG

King City
The Walk
Watch Me Die
My Gun Has Bullets
Dead Space
The Jury Series
Three Ways to Die

The *Diagnosis Murder* Series
The Silent Partner
The Death Merchant
The Shooting Script
The Waking Nightmare
The Past Tense
The Dead Letter
The Double Life
The Last Word

The *Monk* Series
Mr. Monk Goes to the Firehouse
Mr. Monk Goes to Hawaii
Mr. Monk and the Blue Flu
Mr. Monk and the Two Assistants
Mr. Monk in Outer Space
Mr. Monk Goes to Germany
Mr. Monk is Miserable

Mr. Monk and the Dirty Cop
Mr. Monk in Trouble
Mr. Monk is Cleaned Out
Mr. Monk on the Road
Mr. Monk on the Couch
Mr. Monk on Patrol

Non-Fiction
Successful Television Writing
Unsold Television Pilots

Printed in Great Britain
by Amazon